SOLDIER'S SURRENDER

A SWEET MILITARY ROMANCE

HONOR VALLEY ROMANCES
BOOK ONE

SHANAE JOHNSON

It was Aria's favorite day of the year— the first day of summer. The children of Honor Valley would be sleeping in as school had already been out for weeks. Parents would be up early scouring the city paper for activities to engage their children in for the weekend, activities that would hopefully occupy their charges while the parents got a few stolen moments of quiet.

When Aria was a kid, her parents' favorite activity, and her number one choice, was to go to the beach. Although there were no ocean views in the inland state of Montana, the state boasted a number of lakes, rivers, and watersheds offering plenty of water sport and enjoyment. Valor Shore was nestled just to the north of Honor Valley.

In those waters, Aria's father had taught her to swim. On a picnic blanket, she'd shared sandwiches and potato salad with her mom. She'd found her two best friends while playing in the sand. Yes, Valor Shore held all of Aria's best memories, and that was the reason she was going to save its beach.

Aria rolled out of bed just as the first rays of sun were starting to peek over the horizon. She laced up her running shoes, making sure to keep her movements quiet so as not to wake up her roommate, Grace. Once dressed and shoed, Aria set off toward the beach.

The sand was soft and warm beneath her feet. She loved the squish she felt in the soles of her shoes. She pushed herself harder, relishing the feeling of freedom and energy that came with each step.

As she ran, she took in the sights and sounds around her. The waves crashed against the shore, seagulls cried out overhead, and neighbors waved to her as they began their day. Aria felt alive and invigorated, grateful for the beauty of her hometown and the sense of community that she cherished.

The house she'd chosen after she'd come back

from college had been the closest one that she could get to the beach. She went to sleep each night with the sound of the water lapping at the shores. She woke each morning with the smell of… well, not salt. The scent was often unpleasant as the traffic on the beach increased as the weather got warmer.

The joy Aria felt upon waking sank to her toes as she jogged along the shore. Her eyes scanned the sand for a clear path, but all she could see was a mess of plastic bottles, empty snack packets, and other bits of trash littering the once-pristine beach. It was a far cry from the idyllic landscape she remembered from her childhood visits.

She slowed to a stop, feeling a knot of anger and sadness form in her stomach. This was supposed to be a place of natural beauty, a haven for wildlife and humans alike. But instead, it had become a dumping ground for careless visitors and thoughtless litterbugs.

As she stood there, taking in the sight before her, she knew she had to do something. She couldn't just stand by and watch the beach be destroyed. She would have to take action, to rally the community and clean up this precious resource.

Slowing to a walk, Aria bent to pick up a plastic bottle that had washed up on the shore. A pang of disappointment filled her. She had been working tirelessly to organize the annual beach cleanup event. The sight of trash on the beach only strengthened her resolve to make it a success.

With her morning run done, Aria turned her attention to the business at hand. It was a few minutes past seven in the morning. The aroma of fresh coffee beans tickled her nose as she got closer and closer to the coffee shop. Sandy Perk was open and brewing. The morning crew was already at work calling out orders to the early shift of workers in the small town.

"Hey, Aria!" one of the customers called out, waving to her.

"Good morning!" Aria replied, walking behind the counter. It wasn't yet her shift in the café, but she liked showing her face at all times of the day. Being that it was her coffee shop, she knew it was always a good time to make nice with the customers.

She glanced up and smiled as Mr. Johnson, a regular customer, entered the shop. He was a kind-hearted elderly man with a gentle smile and a twinkle in his eyes.

"Morning, Mr. Johnson!" Aria greeted him warmly. "The usual, I assume?"

Mr. Johnson nodded with a chuckle. "You know me too well, Aria. Can't resist your delicious brew."

Aria called out Mr. Johnson's order to Emmie, the barista currently on shift. Then she turned back to Mr. Johnson. "What's on tap for you today, Mr. Johnson? Any exciting plans?"

Mr. Johnson laughed softly. "Oh, nothing too exciting, my dear. Just enjoying the simple pleasures. I was out for a walk on the waters, but I got deterred by all that trash."

Aria nodded empathetically. "Don't worry, Mr. J. I've got a plan for it."

"If it's anything like the plan you had for those beans, I'm sure I'll be back enjoying the sand soon." Mr. Johnson took his travel mug back and found himself a seat near the back of the café.

Aria wanted to assure Mr. Johnson of just that. But she knew better than to make big promises she couldn't deliver on. It was her first year as head of the cleanup, and she had a few things to prove. A few things she *would* prove.

As she turned to head out to get herself properly cleaned up for the afternoon shift, the bell dinged over the door. The dinging bell was obviously a regular occurrence in the coffee shop. But this time, for some reason, the tingling chime caught Aria's attention and urged her to turn around and look.

A man stood in the doorway. In fact, he filled out the doorway. His broad shoulders brushed the sides of the frame. He was tall enough that he had to dip his head lest he bump the bell and make it ring again. Though Aria wasn't sure if it had rung again. The chimes were still ringing in her head.

His sandy blond hair made her think of running carefree along the shore. His bright blue eyes recalled lazy days lying on a beach towel. Aria felt a spark of curiosity and something else, a feeling she couldn't quite identify.

But the guy turned on his heel without even looking at her. A sense of disappointment washed over her. Like she'd just missed out on something. But she couldn't go after it. She had a business to run.

Aria had no idea what made the guy walk out without placing an order. What she did know was that if the new guy wanted a decent cup of coffee, he'd be back. Her café wasn't just the best brew in town, it was the only one.

She took a moment to watch him walk away, noticing his gait and poise. He had the set of a soldier. It was very likely since Honor Valley was the site of a military base. Too bad if he was. Aria had just one rule for her love life, and that was that she didn't date soldiers. No matter if they were as handsome going as they were coming.

CHAPTER TWO

The sun beat down on Jace's bare chest, the sound of the crashing waves filling his ears as he tried to relax on the beach. No matter how hard he tried, he couldn't shake the feeling that he was out of place. His military training had taught him to always be alert and ready for any situation, and the laid-back atmosphere of the small town was making him restless.

Or maybe that was the caffeine withdrawal.

After a lifetime of daily conversations with Morning Joe, Jace had given up the vice last year. He hadn't had a single craving during that time. Until this morning.

Jace had strolled along the sidewalk, the crisp

sea breeze tugging at his hair. He'd been across the street from Sandy Perk, his nose crinkling at the pun. With his nostrils flaring, the tantalizing aroma wafted through the air, capturing his senses and pulling him toward the cozy establishment.

He'd paused, curiosity mingling with temptation. The rich scent of freshly roasted coffee beans triggered memories of early regiments and rituals. His willpower was firmly in place, as it always had been for a seasoned warrior like himself. He could walk away from the bittersweet tang in the air. So why was his hand reaching for the door?

A small voice in his mind reminded him of his commitment to avoid caffeine, but there was something else at play—an unspoken pull, a sense of destiny that beckoned to give the door a tug open. The gentle chime of the bell broke the spell.

Jace let go of the door. It swung firmly closed, taking with it the scent of roasting beans. Something else in the air clung to him as he did an about-face and headed toward the sandy beach.

He was here for rest and relaxation. That was his mission. Now that he was separated from the military, he needed to find a way to fold himself back into the ways of civilian life. Easier said than done since he'd been in training since the tender age of twelve.

Memories of his time in the military academy flooded his mind, both fond and challenging. Twenty years had passed since those formative years, and the impact of that experience still lingered within him.

Fondly, he recalled the camaraderie among his fellow cadets, forged through shared trials and triumphs. The late-night conversations and laughter that echoed through the barracks, the friendships that became his lifeline in a strict and demanding environment. There was a sense of belonging, a unity born out of discipline and mutual respect.

There were also memories that left a bitter taste. The grueling physical training, the relentless drills that pushed them to their limits. The strict regulations and rigid structure that left little room for personal freedom or expression. Jace remembered the moments of exhaustion and frustration, questioning whether the sacrifices he'd made were worth it.

Yet, in the midst of the challenges, Jace couldn't deny the invaluable lessons he had learned. The resilience, discipline, and unwavering determination instilled in him during those years would shape his character for a lifetime. Military school had provided him with the foundation to face adversity head-on and to excel in demanding situations.

The memories evoked a mix of pride and longing. He missed the sense of purpose that came with serving a higher cause, the structure that provided a clear path forward. Now he stood at a crossroads in his life.

Quite literally. There was a cross in his path. A metallic one. It looked like two street signs had been uprooted and banged together. A stop sign, and a sign that read *Dangerous Curves Ahead*. It looked like some teenage prank discarded along the beach.

Jace walked along the shore, his feet sinking into the sand with each step. He tried to focus on the beauty of the waters, but his serenity was continually interrupted by trash and debris. As he strolled along the boardwalk, Jace noticed a few buildings that appeared to be abandoned. He saw a group of teenagers loitering in the corner. He could sense their boredom and frustration. He heard a dog barking in the distance, and he could tell that it was lonely and in need of attention.

Jace's military training had taught him to notice the details, to see the signs of trouble before they became crises. As he looked around the waterfront, Jace noticed the small signs of neglect and decay that suggested the beach was in need of some attention. The right kind of attention.

A notice on the poster board caught his attention. It announced a beach cleanup event this coming weekend. Jace figured if he wanted to relax on the beach, he might as well take part in the cleanup. He longed to be back in service. This seemed an efficient way to hit both his goals.

The notice indicated that the sign-up sheet was located in Sandy Perk. Jace sniffed at that. It would seem that fate had been trying to lead him in the right direction this morning.

He hightailed it back to the main street. This time when the bell dinged, announcing his arrival, Jace didn't turn back. He marched into the café.

Immediately, the warm ambiance embraced him like a refuge from the outside world. The rich aroma of freshly brewed coffee permeated the air, mingling with the comforting scent of pastries and warm bread. Soft jazz music played in the background, adding to the cozy ambiance of the place.

His eyes took in the sight of the cozy seating

areas bathed in warm lighting that created an inviting atmosphere. The walls were adorned with artwork and photographs, likely from locals as it depicted settings and establishments he'd seen in his short time here. The wooden floors creaked softly under his boots as he advanced to the counter, where a chalkboard displayed the daily specials written in colorful, artistic handwriting.

He observed the bustling activity behind the counter as baristas skillfully crafted each cup of coffee with precision and care. The cheerful chatter of customers and the clinking of cups and saucers filled the air, creating a comforting hum of energy. One barista in particular caught his attention.

There was a spark of recognition that made his heart skip a beat. Her warm smile and welcoming presence exuded a sense of genuine hospitality. It was as if they were old friends reuniting after years apart, despite never having met before.

"Excuse me." Jace cleared his throat, hoping to catch the woman's attention amidst the bustling activity. And then he did—capture her attention, that is.

Her gaze fell upon him and held him captive. Her eyes sparkled with a mixture of warmth, drawing him in further. It felt as if she held the key to a world he had been missing.

His gaze lingered on her, unable to tear himself away. In that moment, Jace felt a jolt of connection, an unspoken understanding that seemed to bridge the gap between them. The ringing of the bell announcing a new customer snapped him out of it.

"I'd like to sign up for the beach cleanup." His voice was steady but laced with anticipation.

Her smile widened even further. She looked at him like he was a hero. Jace felt like he'd single-handedly saved the beach with his offer.

"Of course! We'd be delighted to have you join us," she replied, her voice warm and inviting. "Here's the sign-up sheet."

Jace took the sheet. He was careful not to let his fingers touch hers. Something told him that if he did, it'd be like touching a live wire. He was already out of his wits just by looking at this woman.

"My name's Aria. I'm in charge of the cleanup this year."

Jace nodded, holding out the signed sheet for her. His focus remained on holding the paper steady without touching her.

She looked at him expectantly. One brow lifted

as though she'd asked him a question and was waiting for the answer. But he was certain she hadn't said another word. His ears were greedy for that lilting tone in her voice. And then he figured it out.

"Jace. My name's Jace. I'm new in town."

"Soldier?"

"Separated. From the military. Not a woman." Jace closed his mouth to stop it from talking.

Aria's grin only spread wider as she set the paper down. "Can I get you something to drink? On the house for volunteering."

Jace hesitated, unsure of what to order. Coffee was off-limits, but he didn't want to leave just yet. "Surprise me," he said with a slight grin, surrendering to the unknown.

Aria's eyes sparkled with intrigue. As if she knew, she turned to an array of teas, carefully selecting a blend that carried its own unique aroma and charm. Moments later, she placed a steaming cup before him, the scent swirling around him like a gentle embrace.

Jace took a tentative sip, letting the warmth and subtle flavors envelop his senses. The tea felt like a balm, soothing his restless soul. It was different from the coffee he had known, yet equally satisfying.

"Thank you for volunteering," she said. "We don't usually get new recruits."

"I want to be of service, since this is my new home."

Her smile widened again before it closed off. She was holding back with him. Jace wanted to get this woman to open herself to him. Not like she did with the regular customers that came in. He wanted her to open up to him in a way that would let him know her like no one else did. Because right now, he had the urge to tell her things, show her things, that he'd never shared with anyone else.

It had to be the lack of coffee. That's what was muddling his mind. With a nod, he took up his mug. But his feet didn't take him to the door. Instead, he found a table near the back of the café.

Like a covert operator, he sat in the single seat that provided a shadow. Jace savored each sip of tea, his gaze occasionally drifting toward Aria, who attended to other customers with effortless grace. There was a kind of magic in this place, an intangible force that seemed to weave its way into his heart. He sat and sipped and gazed until nothing but calm remained down to his fingertips.

Soon his cup was empty, but somehow, he felt full. Aria glanced up as he strode toward the door. She gave him a smile and a wave, which he returned. Even after he left, the scent of coffee lingered on his clothes. He vowed to return, not just for the tea, but for the possibility of something more—a connection that transcended a simple beverage.

CHAPTER THREE

ria locked the door of her café and took a deep breath, feeling the weight of the day lifting from her shoulders. It was only six in the evening. The sun was still shining and the townsfolk bustling about as their days were coming to an end as well. But she felt like it was the middle of the night after a forty-eight-hour shift.

Being the owner of a bustling business was a good problem to have. Aria knew not every business in town could boast the same issue. Lucky for her, people needed their caffeine fix every day. Sometimes more than once a day.

The thought of caffeine addiction brought her

mind back around to the soldier who'd visited her shop. Jace, he'd said his name was. She was surprised she didn't know his rank and a few of his greatest battle stories as well.

That was her experience with most soldiers. They puffed up their chest and showed off their medals of bravery. More like medals for stupidity.

Aria was all for serving country and community. But some of the young soldiers that passed through Honor Valley treated service more like a video game they could score points in than the life-changing event it was for the people they served. It left them with an inflated ego and a hero complex they couldn't see past.

It hadn't appeared that way with Jace, whose last name and rank she did not know. The fact that he wanted to help was another thing she hadn't seen coming. What she had seen were the worry lines pulling at the edges of his eyes. She'd seen the groves at the corners of his mouth where his lips rested in a frown that seemed permanently carved into his face.

Yet he'd smiled at her. It hadn't been a big smile. It had seemed like work. It had seemed like the facial expression had surprised him more than anything.

A smile like that, with eyes like those, needed more serenity. Hence, the tea mixture of lavender, chamomile, and vanilla.

She'd gotten that one right. She could tell as he sat in the back of the café. His shoulders had relaxed. His gaze had softened. True, his eyes kept coming back and resting on her. But that was all she'd let them do; rest on her. She was not going to let that gaze go anywhere further or take her with him.

"You would not believe the day I had."

Aria turned to spot her friend Grace coming up from the other end of the street where the town library was housed.

"It's going to have to wait until you hear about mine," said Sarah, coming from next door where she worked at the flower shop.

Grace, Sarah, and Aria had been friends right out of the womb. They lived on the same block. Each had birthdays in the summer, meaning their parties were never a class affair. And they'd each chosen to stay in the small town they loved after college.

"The city council is considering getting rid of the after-school reading program." Grace put her hands on her hips, stretching the cardigan she wore over a lacy blouse.

"That stinks, Gracie. But you wait 'til you hear who's coming to my family reunion." Sarah paused for dramatic effect. She'd pursued drama in high school, but found her calling arranging bouquets in the flower shop. "My ex and…" She held up a finger for dramatic effect. "His new fiancée."

"No," Grace and Aria sighed at the same time.

"This calls for ice cream," said Aria. "Double scoops all around."

Linking arms with her two best friends, Aria treated the duo to Neapolitan ice cream with sprinkles and fudge at the town creamery. She let her friends wax on about their personal lives. Her meeting today with the new soldier in town she kept to herself. It wasn't like anything would come of it.

And she was right.

She'd expected Jace to come into the café on the next day. But he was MIA. Her eyes scanned the gathering crowd on the beach, searching for any sign of Jace. Her heart fluttered with a mix of anticipation and uncertainty, unsure if he would actually show up for the beach cleanup.

And then, amidst the bustling activity, she

spotted him. Jace emerged from the distance, walking with purpose toward her. Time seemed to slow as her breath caught in her throat. Her heart skipped a beat, a rush of excitement coursing through her veins.

He looked resolute, his strides confident, as if he had a clear purpose in mind. The sunlight played off his rugged features, emphasizing the strength and determination etched upon them. Aria's eyes traced the lines of his face, the way his short-cropped hair caught the gentle breeze, adding to his rugged charm.

Her emotions were a tumultuous mix of longing and hesitation. Her past experiences had left her wary of getting involved with soldiers, the unpredictability and heartache that often accompanied their lives. But seeing Jace walking toward her, the walls she had built around her heart trembled, threatening to crumble.

Aria's grip tightened on the clipboard in her hand, her knuckles turning white. She reminded herself of her resolve, the need to protect her own heart. She couldn't let herself be vulnerable again, not with someone who carried the weight of the military on his shoulders.

Still, her heartbeat quickened, echoing the

sound of the crashing waves nearby. With every step he took, the distance between them closed, and Aria braced herself for the whirlwind of emotions that awaited her.

When he finally reached her side, the small smile he'd worn a couple of days ago had grown wider on his face. Only slightly, but because the vision of the first hard-won smile had been etched in her memory, she clocked the growth.

"Hey," she greeted him, her voice filled with a mix of excitement and vulnerability. "I'm glad you made it."

"Wouldn't miss it," he said. "I figured I'd start at the farthest edge of the beach. Maybe take a few young men with me to get started."

Aria blinked, feeling the spray of cold water on her face. "I haven't given out assignments yet."

Jace glanced down at the clipboard cradled in her arms. The list of assignments was facing outwards. She caught the quick flicker of his eyes as he took in her typed notes from top to bottom.

"Are you sure this is the most efficient way to do it?" he said. "It seems like we could save a lot of time if we split up into smaller groups and focused on specific areas."

Aria raised an eyebrow, surprised by Jace's boldness. She had been a part of this cleanup for years. True, this would be her first time in charge, but she had seen its success. And that success had always been done this way.

"Interesting idea," she said slowly. "But we've always done it this way, and it's worked pretty well in the past."

"I've done my fair share of military operations, and I know a thing or two about efficient logistics."

Aria's heart sank as Jace pushed back on her plans for the beach cleanup event. She knew it was important to get everyone on board with the assigned tasks to make sure everything got done efficiently and effectively. But Jace was not backing down.

"It doesn't make sense to have people do tasks they're not comfortable with," she said. "It's best to let people choose what they want to do."

"That's less efficient. Some people are just doing things to hang out with their friends."

"That's why they show up," she pointed out. "It's community building."

"I thought the point was to clean up, not hang out with friends."

"The point in community building is always to hang out with friends."

Jace opened his mouth like he wanted to argue but then closed it.

Aria bit her lip, feeling frustrated. She had spent countless hours organizing the event and felt like her efforts were being questioned. But she also knew that Jace was trying to help, and she didn't want to push him away. She needed those big, strong hands to carry the heavy load from down at the far end of the beach.

"Look, I appreciate your input," Aria said, trying to keep her voice calm. "But I think it's best if we stick to the plan."

Jace looked like he wanted to argue more, but he ultimately sighed and nodded. "Fine, I'll go with your way," he said, still sounding grumpy.

Aria smiled, relieved that the tension had dissipated. "Thank you, Jace. You'll see, this will go smoothly."

"Where do you want me?"

The question made her cheeks color. She pointed to the dunes, which happened to be the farthest end of the beach, exactly where he'd recommended placing himself. Jace nodded and headed that way.

As they walked away from each other, Aria felt a flutter in her chest. There was something about Jace that drew her in, despite their disagreements. She shook her head, trying to push the thought aside. There was work to be done.

CHAPTER FOUR

*J*ace shouldn't have said that to her, but it was exactly what he meant. Where did Aria want him? Because that's where she could have him.

He'd stayed away for the past couple of days because he knew the fact of those words before she'd ever voiced them. Though technically he hadn't stayed away. He just hadn't gone into the café.

He'd loitered across the street in the library, pretending to browse the shelves but all the while sneaking glances across the street into the café window. The scent of old books filled his nostrils, momentarily overpowering the lingering aroma of coffee. He tried to distract himself by perusing the shelves, running his fingers over the spines of well-worn novels, but his mind wandered back to Aria and the calming tea she had made for him.

He'd put his nose in a bouquet of flowers outside the flower shop as he desperately tried to ignore the tempting aroma of freshly brewed coffee that wafted through the air, emanating from Aria's café. It teased his senses, evoking memories of their encounter and the undeniable connection they shared. The memory stirred a longing within him, a desire to be by her side and experience those quiet moments of solace together.

Jace continued to dance on the periphery, caught between the enticing scent of coffee and the knowledge that he was not yet relationship material. Not when he still hadn't quite figured out how to blend back into civilian life even in this quiet, slow-paced town.

What he could do was help clean up the beach for her. And so he went where Aria directed him to go, which was the farthest stretch of the beach away from her. Because he'd blown it. Just like he knew he would.

For a man who had been under command as well as in command for most of his life, he still had trouble turning that part of his brain off. But he couldn't help himself. He was used to being in charge and looking for gaps in a mission plan.

His analytical mind had saved many lives. Only now it wasn't about saving a life. It was about helping this community.

The sun was shining brightly, and Jace was glad to be there, despite his initial reservations. He felt a little overwhelmed by the number of people around him. There were families with young kids, teenagers in groups, and older adults, all wearing gloves and carrying trash bags.

His gaze kept sliding back to Aria in the distance. It was clear she was in charge, walking around with that clipboard and a determined look on her face. He hadn't made the best impression this morning, but he was resolved to put in the best effort of all the workers today to impress the woman in command.

Jace found that he wasn't alone on his portion of the beach. Michael, a young man around his own age, had been assigned this area as well. They introduced themselves and quickly got to work, picking up trash and debris with ease.

As they worked, Jace began to see the value in Aria's plan. It was well thought out and efficient, and it was clear that she had put a lot of effort into organizing the event. He felt a little embarrassed for doubting her. The effort was moving swiftly and efficiently, like clockwork.

"Are you stationed at the base?" Michael asked as he held a bag open for Jace.

"I'm recently separated." Jace opened his mouth to explain that the separation was from the military and not a marriage, but Michael nodded in understanding.

The base was situated on the edge of the town, so it made sense that most people would understand the lingo. Including people like Aria, who he'd mansplained the term to the other day. Though Jace had been less patronizing and simply tongue-tied by the woman's presence.

"This event is run pretty well," Jace said, trying to find a way to hedge into learning more about the event's organizer.

"Yeah, Aria Reynolds is in charge this year," Michael volunteered. "She's been volunteering for the cleanups since we were kids. Her mom and dad spent a lot of time on the beach before they passed away. So the beach holds a special place in her heart."

"You seem to know her well." Jace's voice was clipped and his gaze shrewd as he took in

Michael's measure. The man didn't notice as he bent down to pick up a piece of plastic.

"Yeah, she's always been like a sister to me. She's dedicated to this town and its people."

Jace nodded. "I can see that. She's organized this event well."

Michael chuckled. "Yeah, that's Aria for you. She's always been a bit of a control freak, but she gets things done."

More and more of the beach's beauty was unveiled as the layers of trash went into dark bags. The sound of crashing waves and seagulls filled the air. Michael had gone quiet, focusing on the task at hand. Jace gave the silence a few more seconds before filling it.

"I stopped in for a drink in her café the other day. It was the best cup of tea I've ever had. In fact, I think it's the only cup of tea I've ever had."

"Yeah, Aria has poured her heart into that place. It's all she had left after her divorce."

Jace's ears perked up at that. Divorce? All she had left? Those two statements didn't go together in his mind. Had her ex-husband tried to take her livelihood from her? What kind of man would do that?

"Her ex was a soldier," Michael continued.

"They got married young, right out of high school. But he came back from overseas with some trauma, and they couldn't work through it."

"Was he… dangerous to her?"

Michael looked up at Jace as if finally remembering that he was talking to another living soul. "I probably shouldn't speak out of turn."

The man had been spilling his guts for the last quarter hour.

"I wasn't trying to pry." Though that was exactly what Jace had been doing.

"I can tell you that she's not into soldiers anymore. Her ex left a bad taste in her mouth."

Jace's mouth opened to deny he had that kind of interest in Aria. The kick to his chest from the inside and Michael's raised eyebrow told him that he wouldn't be believed if he uttered those words.

"You're new in town," Michael went on. "Honor Valley is a very welcoming place, but we look after our own."

Translation: Jace might live here now, but he wasn't yet a trusted member of town. He wasn't an insider. That, coupled with the notion that he was a soldier, wouldn't win him any favors with the woman he couldn't stop thinking about.

Though Jace didn't suffer from any major

PTSD symptoms, he still was having trouble adjusting to civilian life. Maybe it would be for the best to leave Aria Reynolds alone.

The sound of raucous laughter and glass breaking tore Jace's attention away from his task. A trio of college-aged males were slinging pebbles at beer bottles. Their poor aim missed most shots, but two of the bottles shattered. The group, oblivious to the significance of the cleanup event, seemed to find amusement in leaving a trail of trash in their wake.

Jace's jaw tightened, and a flicker of anger sparked in his eyes. "Hey, you need to clean that up."

The group paused, their laughter fading as they locked eyes with Jace's piercing gaze. For a moment, there was hesitation in their expressions, a glimpse of realization, and surprise that their actions had consequences.

One of the individuals, attempting to mask their guilt with bravado, sneered and replied, "What's it to you, soldier boy? You gonna make us?"

Jace's jaw clenched, his voice firm but measured. "I won't ask again. Either you pick up your trash and contribute to the betterment of this community, or you'll have me to deal with."

His words hung in the air, the weight of his military training and inner resolve palpable. The group glanced at each other, a hint of uncertainty flickering in their eyes. Slowly, begrudgingly, they began to gather the litter they had callously scattered.

Satisfied, Jace turned back to Michael. The man had a raised brow and a half smile on his face. Neither spoke of it, as men were wont to do. However, a glance down the beach showed that Michael wasn't the only one who had caught Jace chastising the students.

He looked over to find Aria watching him, her clipboard lowered, the pen resting on her full bottom lip. In her eyes, he saw a glimmer of admiration, and his chest swelled.

CHAPTER FIVE

Aria stood at the bed of the truck that would take all the trash collected away. By all accounts, the cleanup was a raging success. The fact that people got to spend time with friends and that it was in some cases a family affair had been a hit. It had all gone off without a hitch until she saw the rowdy college kids making a mess at the far end of the beach.

She'd been about to march over to the bottle breakers herself when she saw Jace move in. From the first moment, Aria could only admire the command in him.

That square set to his shoulders. That focus in his narrowed gaze. She'd found it deeply attractive, but also unsettling.

It was unsettling because it reminded her of Troy. The gentle breeze felt both comforting and suffocating, as memories of her failed marriage filled the air like whispers of a lost love.

Aria closed her eyes, trying to shut out the flood of emotions that threatened to overwhelm her. The weight of her past relationship with her ex-husband, a soldier she'd once loved deeply, pressed heavily on her heart. They had shared dreams and aspirations, but somewhere along the way, the effects of his PTSD had taken hold, eroding the connection they'd once had.

Images of happier times flashed before her eyes —laughter, embraces, and stolen moments of tenderness. Those moments were overshadowed by the pain of witnessing the slow unraveling of the man she had vowed to spend her life with. She had seen the light fade from his eyes, replaced by an emptiness that she couldn't reach.

Tears welled up in Aria's eyes, her fingers clutching the orderly clipboard in her arms as if seeking solace. The ache in her chest grew with each passing memory as she realized how their love had become a casualty of the very war he had fought.

In times like these, she questioned herself,

wondering if she could have done more, if she could have been stronger, more understanding. But deep down, she knew it wasn't about her strength or devotion. It was about the demons that haunted him, the unseen wounds that tore at his soul, rendering him a stranger within his own skin.

Aria's mind was a battlefield of conflicting emotions—the love she still carried for the man he had once been, intertwined with the pain of the shattered dreams they had shared. She had come to terms with the fact that sometimes love was not enough to heal the wounds inflicted by war.

Taking a deep breath, Aria resolved to focus on the present. She had been through the depths of heartache and understood the toll it could take, but she refused to let it define her future. And that's when Jace appeared again in her vision.

He didn't take a step toward the messy college kids. He simply stood his ground, his arms crossed, his stance full of command. She could see the young men bristle. Saw them rear up, then immediately back down. Not only did they back down, but they bent down and began cleaning up their mess. All without any physical altercations.

Aria blinked a few more times. What had just happened?

Whenever Troy was confronted with a problem, he'd dealt with it physically. Another guy looking at Aria—that would end with a fist to the guy's eye. Money problems—he would go down to the bank and shout at the teller. Steak medium instead of medium rare—well, there were restaurants in town Aria was still ashamed to show her face at.

But Jace? He hadn't even raised his voice. And it looked like the problem was dealt with.

He'd said he was a soldier, hadn't he? Maybe he hadn't seen combat? Maybe his time in the service hadn't broken him like it had her ex-husband?

Aria watched Jace from a distance as he worked tirelessly with the other volunteers to clean up the beach. She couldn't help but worry that her strong personality might be intimidating him. She knew that she could come across as bossy and overbearing, and she didn't want to scare him off.

As she made her way over to where Jace was working, she tried to soften her approach. "Hey, how's it going?" she asked with a smile.

Jace looked up from his work and returned the

smile. "Good, we're making some real progress here."

Aria nodded, relieved that he seemed at ease. "I'm glad you're enjoying yourself. I know this isn't exactly the most glamorous work, but it's important."

Jace nodded in agreement. "Yeah, it feels good to be making a difference. I've spent so much time overseas in villages and shanty towns trying to help better people's lives. It feels really good to be back home on my country's soil and doing something directly for the people of a community."

Aria had no words for him. He'd confirmed he'd been overseas, in war zones, if the mention of shanty towns was something to go by. But he wasn't brazen, and he wasn't boasting. She had no idea what to make of him.

As she stood there dumb and mute, a commotion sounded from the trucks. The trash hadn't been secured in the back when the driver took off. The truck went one way and the trash bags the other. All of the trash that had been collected spilled into a heap on the ground.

To make matters worse, the wind started to kick up, and the trash began to billow out, trying to return to where it had been originally discarded.

All of their hard work was getting away from them. Volunteers rushed around, trying to keep everything under control, but it was too much to handle.

Aria's heart sank as she looked around at the mess. She knew that this setback would delay the cleanup effort and cause more harm to the environment. She stood frozen, trying to figure out how to handle the matter.

"Are you okay?" Jace asked, placing a hand on her shoulder.

"No, I'm not. This is a disaster. All of our work has gone to waste."

Jace scanned the beach, taking in the chaos. "Don't worry, we can handle this. We'll just have to work a little harder."

"But how?" Aria asked, her voice filled with despair.

Jace took charge, quickly organizing a plan of action. He divided the volunteers into smaller groups and instructed each group to focus on a specific section of the beach. The younger men he sent to the farther reaches. For the elderly and children, he set up a parameter around the truck where most of the trash had fallen.

It was his original plan. Surprisingly, It worked.

Aria watched in amazement as Jace's military training came into play. He barked out orders with precision, and the volunteers responded immediately. The trash was collected quickly and returned to the bags. This time, Jace secured the collection in the back of the truck himself. A cheer went up as the truck pulled off with the trash in tow.

Aria turned to Jace, feeling grateful for his quick thinking. "Thank you," she said. "I don't know what we would have done without you."

"I know this isn't how you planned for things to go, but sometimes life throws curveballs. It's up to us to handle them."

He was right. She couldn't let setbacks defeat her. She had to keep moving forward.

"Thank you for letting me help today," he continued. "I've been feeling…" He sighed, searching for the words. "I'm trying to find my place in the world now that I'm back on this side of it. It felt good to be a part of something again."

"Well, I was thinking, maybe I could thank you properly," Aria said, feeling her heart race. "Maybe a cup of coffee? On me, of course."

Her heart plummeted into her stomach when she saw his hesitation.

"I gave up coffee," he said.

"Oh. Tea, then? I make a great calming tea."

"Yes, you do."

That didn't sound like a yes. It didn't feel like a yes. Had Aria misread the signals? She hadn't dated anyone since her divorce. Before that, she hadn't dated at all. Troy had been her only. Her everything.

"You know what, just come into the café anytime and grab that tea." She was already backing away from him, from the offer, from the possibility. She turned to the crowd at large. "In fact, the next drink is on me for everyone who volunteered today."

A cheer went up in the crowd. Her friends and neighbors surrounded her, clapping her on the back for her hospitality and leadership. As they closed around her, she lost sight of Jace.

*J*ace sat on the sand, watching the waves roll in and out. His hands were loosely clasped around his knees as he stared out at the vast expanse of water before him. The beach was clean, pristine even, a stark contrast to the disarray he'd found it in earlier before the cleanup event. It was a small victory, but one he felt deeply.

The sun beat down on his skin, but he hardly felt it. His mind was restless, as it often was these days. He couldn't shake the feeling that he was meant to be doing something more, something bigger.

It would still be weeks before he started his new job on the military base in Honor Valley. Until then, his orders were to relax, decompress, relearn how to be a member of society outside of the confines of a unit.

Easier said than done.

As he listened to the rhythmic crash of the waves, his mind wandered back to his time in the military, to the missions he'd undertaken and the scars he bore. They weren't all visible, these scars. Some were etched deep within, invisible to the eye but ever present in his mind. A constant reminder of the life he had once led, of the choices he had made.

Unlike some of his comrades, he hadn't turned to drugs or destructive habits to cope with the aftermath of war. He hadn't contemplated ending his life. But the restlessness, the inability to truly relax, clung to him like a stubborn shadow, following him even in the quiet tranquility of this cozy, close-knit small town.

The seagulls cawed overhead, their flight a dance against the backdrop of the rising sun. Jace closed his eyes, letting the sounds of the ocean and the distant call of the birds fill his senses. His muscles, aching from the day's work, relaxed as he sank deeper into his thoughts.

He thought about the years he had spent

serving his country, the friends he had made, and the ones he had lost. He remembered the adrenaline rush of each mission, the sense of purpose, the camaraderie. He also remembered the fear, the uncertainty, the moments of sheer terror that had forever changed him.

Now, far removed from the battlefield, he found himself in a different kind of fight. A struggle to find peace, to quiet the restlessness that buzzed under his skin. A fight to fit into a world that felt alien, despite being back on home soil.

Opening his eyes, he looked at the clean beach once more. Yesterday had been spent clearing away trash, restoring the beauty of the place. It was a humble task, yet satisfying in a way his military victories had never been. It was tangible proof that he could make a difference, that he could heal a small part of the world, just as he was trying to heal himself.

The footsteps coming up behind him didn't make him jolt. They were too evenly paced. Too sure of themselves. They belonged to soldiers like him.

Two shadows fell over him. He looked up, shielding his eyes. Even though they stood backlit in the sunlight, he'd know Alex and Mason anywhere. Two fellow soldiers, two brothers he'd shared more than just a battlefield with.

"Mind if we join you?" Alex asked, gesturing to the sand beside Jace.

He shrugged, shifting over slightly to make room for his friends. They settled on either side of him, a trio of former soldiers seeking solace on the quiet beach before families and rabble rousers stole the tranquility away.

They sat in silence for a time. Only the rhythmic lull of the waves spoke. The three knew enough about one another that they didn't need to bother with the small chat.

Mason could have sat in stillness all day so long as he had a book in his hand. It was Alex that was the first to break the silence.

"It's not fair, you know," Alex grumbled, digging his toes into the sand. "Just because I'm not married doesn't mean I'm going to up and leave town."

Alex was the ambitious one. Always looking for the next promotion, the next step up the ladder. But his bachelor status had become an unexpected hurdle. The base commander believed a family man was more likely to stick around, but Alex wasn't one to settle down, not yet.

"You've always been committed," said Jace. "The commander will see that, married or not."

"Wait? Did you say that he always should've been committed?" joked Mason.

Alex reached behind Jace to give the other man a punch on the shoulder. But Mason, being the trained soldier that he was, dodged the jab.

Mason turned his face, showing the visible scars he'd brought back with him from his time in the service. He spent most of his time in the library, his nose buried in a book. Jace and Alex often teased him that it was the librarian he was really interested in, not the books. But like the two of them, a relationship was not the best card to play right now.

Aria's bright smile shone in Jace's mind just then. The invitation to have a drink on the house rang in his ears. She'd been trying to ask him out. Until she'd gotten scared. Jace had seen the moment of the transition from hope to fear. Because he'd felt it right alongside her.

"You ever think about asking her out?" Jace began, breaking the silence. "The librarian, I mean."

Mason's cheeks reddened slightly, his eyes focused on the horizon. "I like the quiet," he said finally. "The books. It's...calming."

Jace smiled softly. He understood. They were all seeking peace in their own way. He, too, was searching, and he thought he saw a piece of it in Aria.

"I met someone," he found himself saying. His friends turned to look at him, surprise etched on their faces. Jace laughed, rubbing the back of his neck. "Her name's Aria. She's... different. I can't really explain it."

Mason and Alex exchanged a glance. A glance between soldiers spoke volumes. With just a look, they could communicate the presence of danger or security. The look his friends shared clearly said to proceed with caution.

"I don't know," Jace went on. "When I'm around her, I just feel… calm." He searched for more words to describe his reaction to Aria. "Settled. Content."

Mason and Alex shared another look. This one Jace couldn't read because the two men looked confused.

"So what's the plan?" Mason asked.

"Did you ask her out?" Alex asked.

Jace shook his head. "Her ex suffered from PTSD. I gathered it was hard for her, and it didn't end well. I don't think she'd date me even if I asked."

"And you're worried you might' go down the same path?" asked Mason.

Jace focused on the horizon, staring directly into the sun. "I have my own demons. I'm not sure it's fair to ask her to deal with them, too."

"We all have our issues," Alex said, his voice firm. "That doesn't mean we don't deserve happiness."

"But what if—"

"No 'what ifs,'" Alex interrupted. "You can't predict the future. You can't let fear of what might happen stop you from living your life."

Jace glanced at his friends. Alex, always striving for more but held back by an unfair standard. Mason, hiding his pain behind books and the quiet solitude of the library. And him, scared to let someone in because of the constant restlessness in his body.

He thought of Aria, her smile, the way she seemed to see him—the real him, not just the soldier. Was it worth the risk? Could he bear to put her through what she had already experienced once before?

"You won't know unless you try," Alex said, as if reading Jace's thoughts. "And remember, you're not alone. You've got us. And if Aria's as special as you say she is, she'll understand."

Jace was silent, considering his friends' words. The sun was fully in the sky now. Beachgoers were starting to arrive with their blankets and floaties. Jace sat still, thinking of Aria, of the possibility of something more. Of happiness, fear, pain, and hope.

ria had never hosted a community forum in her café before, but she was excited to see so many people turn up. The scent of coffee mixed with the chatter of people filled the air as she made her way around the room, greeting everyone and making sure they had a hot beverage in hand. Some of the townsfolk were voicing serious issues, while others brought up light-hearted topics.

She glanced over at Grace, who was engaging the elementary school principal about the need of the library reading program. Or maybe he was engaging her. Either way, the two were preaching to the choir about the necessity of getting the town's children's reading levels up.

Sarah was trying to get away from the butcher's son, whose gaze kept slipping to her chest instead of her face as he talked. Sarah's lips didn't move at all, while her unwanted suitor's lips kept flapping. But she couldn't get away. Not when her mother blocked her on one end and her aunt blocked her on the other. They were determined to see her happily married before the end of the year, whether she liked it or not.

"I'm telling you, the trash situation is out of control," said Mr. Johnson, a retired fisherman. "Every day I'm out on the water, and I see more and more debris floating by. We need to do something about it."

"I agree," said Mrs. Wilson, the owner of one of the two inns in town. "And what about the potholes on Main Street? They're getting worse every year."

"And what about the lack of affordable housing?" chimed in a young couple who had just moved to town. "We can barely afford to pay rent on our apartment, let alone think about buying a house."

Typically, problems like this were addressed at the monthly town halls. But Aria had noted during the beach cleanup that a constant topic of conversation was the need for improvements in their small town.

She kept hearing these sentiments in the days following the cleanup as people came in to snag the free beverage she'd promised anyone who worked on the event that day. So she decided to hold an open forum. The forum also helped her to recoup the costs of her impromptu free round of drinks. With everyone on their first or second paid cup of Joe, Aria was back in the black. The only person who hadn't come into get their free drink was the one she'd initially made the offering to.

She had to face facts; she'd scared Jace away. First with her bossy attitude, then with her mixed signals.

The sound of the chime over the door signaled the arrival of a latecomer. The door to the café swung open, and Aria's eyes were drawn to the figure standing in the doorway. It was Jace. Aria's heart skipped a beat as she took in his rugged appearance, but she quickly composed herself and walked over to him.

"Jace, what brings you here?" she asked, trying to sound casual.

Unlike the butcher's son, Jace's eyes stayed locked on Aria's. She almost wished they'd slip down inappropriately to her chest. It would be the only way to break the spell.

But he did not let her go. In fact, he stepped closer to her until he filled her vision and her nostrils. He'd brought the smell of the beach with him.

"You promised me a cup of tea."

His deep voice pressed in on Aria, making her want to curl up into his strong chest.

"I've come to collect."

She knew her head was nodding. But she couldn't get her feet to work. What was it about this man that made her want to step closer to him?

He was a soldier. That should have been warning enough to steer clear. Her experience with her husband had truly left its mark on her.

But still, Aria knew not all soldiers dealt with their issues the way her ex-husband had. Jace hadn't given a single indicator that he might lose his temper. He gave every indication that he was self-possessed and level-headed. Which was more than she could say for Troy before he had gone into the military.

"I didn't realize you were… busy." Jace looked around at the group and then back at Aria.

"You're more than welcome to be here. We're just discussing some community issues."

Aria rounded the counter, placing some distance between herself and the magnetic pull to Jace. He followed, settling himself on a stool as she worked. The counter was little match for the attraction between them.

"What issue is the community facing other than trash on the beach?" he asked.

"Normal things you might face in a small town." Aria packed the herbs in the infuser before settling the device in the tea mug. "What do you think about the proposal to add more bike lanes in town?"

"I think it's a great idea. It'll promote a healthier lifestyle and reduce traffic on the roads while also reducing carbon emissions. However, it's important to make sure that the bike lanes are implemented safely and thoughtfully. Sometimes lanes can take up parking spots and hurt businesses."

Aria wasn't sure what she'd expected from his response. The level of thoughtfulness stunned her so much that she let the water in his teacup spill over. She wasn't the only one intrigued by Jace's opinions. Many of the townsfolk gathered turned to him. A few came up to him and asked his opinion on other matters.

Just like his well-rounded response to the bike matter, Jace discussed the pros and cons of the reading program with Grace, the pothole conundrum with Mrs. Wilson, and even managed to lure the butcher's son away from Sarah to discuss the latest sports game from the weekend.

Jace did all of this from his seat at the counter. His shoulders had been erect when he'd turned sideways to come into the café. As he sipped his tea, he relaxed more and more.

Aria had been walking around the café tending to her customers. But like the magnet he was to her, she stayed by his side. Finding a clean spot to run a rag over. Topping off his mug with more water.

One by one, her customers began to file out. Grace and Sarah were two of the last to leave, each of her friends casting covert glances and Sarah making goo-goo eyes and kissy faces behind Jace's back.

And then finally, they were alone. Jace's mug was empty. He covered the top with his hand when Aria lifted the teapot.

"I'm glad you came," Aria said, breaking the

silence. "You have some really good advice. You'll be a benefit to the town."

"Thank you for saying so. I'm finding it hard to fit back into civilian life."

"Yeah? How so?"

"Just… restless. Except when I'm near you."

Aria tried to fight it, tried to resist the pull she felt toward him. But every time their eyes met, every time he smiled at her, she found herself falling a little more.

"But I suppose that's because you keep plying me with calming teas." He pushed the mug toward her and then locked gazes with her once more. "The truth is that I'm interested in being near you, Aria."

Aria hadn't let another man get near her. The memories of her failed marriage were still too fresh, the wounds still raw. She wasn't sure if she was ready to take that risk again.

"Aria, would you like to go out with me sometime?"

CHAPTER EIGHT

*J*ace arrived at Aria's doorstep, dressed in a dark suit that he hoped was appropriate for their date. Though maybe he should have gone more casual. A suit was probably too formal for a night out in a small town. Though they weren't staying in town. Jace planned to drive them thirty minutes away into the next town over, which was much more metropolitan. So maybe the suit was the right call?

He didn't have time to stress over it any longer. As soon as Aria opened the door, he was struck by how beautiful she looked. Jace watched as Aria approached, a slow smile playing on his lips. He was captivated by her, his gaze drawn to her like a moth to a flame. From his perspective, she was the embodiment of elegance and grace, her simple dress showcasing her natural beauty.

The dress, a soft shade of lavender, hugged her figure modestly, its silhouette simple yet flattering. The subtle floral pattern on the fabric whispered of spring and renewal, reflecting the hope he felt blossoming in his heart. The dress accentuated her curves, falling just above her knee, lending her an air of understated elegance.

Her dark hair was pulled back into a loose bun, tendrils escaping to frame her face. The setting sun cast a warm glow on her skin, highlighting the soft blush on her cheeks. Her eyes, always expressive and vibrant, sparkled with anticipation. Her lips, painted a light rose, were curved into a shy smile, radiating warmth and inviting him in.

Jace stepped closer. Stepped or was pulled, he wasn't sure. He didn't care. He was prepared to follow this woman to the ends of the earth if she'd let him.

"Wow," he breathed, his eyes lingering on her for a moment too long. "You look absolutely stunning, Aria."

"Thank you, Jace. You look pretty handsome yourself."

Jace's heart raced at her compliment. In that

moment, he knew he'd made the right decision with the suit. He wanted nothing more than to kiss her right then and there. But he knew it was too soon, and instead, he offered her his arm and led her to his car.

As they drove to the restaurant, Jace stole glances at Aria. The way the setting sun illuminated her face, the way her hair blew in the wind through the open window. It all made him feel alive. Peaceful. Settled.

His foot didn't tap against the floorboard of the car as the traffic slowed them down. His mind wasn't racing ahead to tomorrow and making lists of what needed to be done, along with a Plan B, C, and D for contingencies if Plan A went wrong. He was completely in the moment, tuned in to the woman sitting next to him.

"You know," he finally said, breaking the comfortable silence between them, "I was nervous to ask you out."

"I know," she said. "I was nervous to say yes."

"I know."

Jace smiled at her, the feeling of nervousness and excitement growing inside him. This was a chance to get to know Aria on a deeper level, to see if there was a real connection between them. He was determined to make this date a night to remember.

The restaurant was cozy and intimate, the perfect setting for a romantic dinner. As they sat down, Jace took a deep breath and tried to steady his racing heart. The woman sitting across from him had pulled all of his attention, but now that he was settled in his seat, he began to take in more of his setting.

It was a busy night, and the restaurant was crowded. Though he had a good line of sight to the exits, they were sitting in the middle of the commotion. Jace had trouble not scratching the itch to constantly glance over his shoulder. He could feel the anxiety building inside him, the noise and movement of the people around him making him feel like he was back in the war zone. But he didn't want to show weakness in front of Aria. He knew that any notion that he still carried any trauma with him would change her mind.

Aria, being the perceptive woman that she was, noticed. She reached out to gently touch his hand. "Are you okay, Jace?"

Jace forced a smile. "Yeah, I'm fine. Just not used to being around so many people."

"I understand that crowds can be over-whelming for you."

They hadn't been the other day in her café, which had been packed with townsfolk. True, he'd met many of them during the beach cleanup event. That had been a bit crowded, too. But he'd been in a wide-open space as people had introduced them-selves, and he'd gotten to know them on an indi-vidual basis, like Michael. They were in the next town over, and none of these faces were familiar.

Still, Jace felt a wave of relief wash over him, grateful that Aria could see through his façade. He took a few more deep breaths, focusing on her comforting touch. Her fingers remained on his, and Jace began to feel a sense of calm, like a warm blanket wrapping around him.

Though her fingers were a bit stiff. Her eyes darted here and there around the restaurant, as though her mind were somewhere else. The air was charged between them, but he felt a polarity shift.

"You love to be in a crowd, though. That's why you run a café and organize community events."

"I love to be in my community," Aria corrected, taking her hand back as the waiter arrived with their main courses. "I've known the people there since I was born. They're my family."

"I only knew the men and women in my unit for a fraction of my life. But I would trust each and every one of them with my life. And they would say the same."

"People change, though. I knew my ex-husband all of my life, and he changed right before my eyes."

Her eyes went distant again. Looking back into a past where Jace couldn't reach her. He was in the midst of asking her more about the community forum to change the topic when it happened.

A loud crash cut through the restaurant. It was the unmistakable sound of a tray hitting the floor, the clatter of silverware echoing like a burst of gunfire, followed by a few yelps of surprise as diners shuffled in their chairs to move out of the way.

Jace's muscles tensed, his body reacting instinctively to the sudden, jarring noise. His eyes darted to the source of the sound, a young waiter who had dropped his tray, his face red with embarrassment. Instead of going on full alert or rising from his seat to protect the precious asset sitting across from him, Jace took a deep breath and steadied himself.

He turned back to Aria, ready to launch back into their conversation but stopped when he saw the panic in her eyes. She had gone pale, her hands trembling slightly as she looked at him with a mix of fear and concern. She was reacting not to the crash itself, but to what she feared it might do to him. Or what she'd experienced in the past with her ex-husband.

Jace reached across the table, covering her trembling hand with his. "Aria," he said, his voice steady and calm. "It's okay."

"The sound... I thought it might..." She trailed off, her words choked by her worry. Her eyes searched his, looking for some kind of sign.

Jace squeezed her hand gently. "Everything's okay, I promise."

She let him lace his fingers with hers. It did not stop hers from trembling.

CHAPTER NINE

As the clatter echoed through the restaurant, Aria felt a shiver of dread creep up her spine. It was a sound that she knew all too well, a trigger that could turn a peaceful moment into a nightmare. She braced herself, preparing for the worst.

In her mind's eye, she saw flashes of her past—her ex-husband's face contorting into a mask of fear, his body trembling, his voice raised in a shout that sent chills down her spine. It was a scene she had witnessed more times than she cared to remember, a scene that had left deep scars on her heart.

There was a part of her heart that still belonged to Troy. It always would. But the man that he was, the man she'd fallen in love with, was not who he was today. By the time their marriage was over, he wasn't even trying. She had had to come to grips with the fact that he never would try. He'd let his demons get too deep of a hold on him.

Aria's gaze flew to Jace, her breath hitching in her throat. Instead of the panic she was expecting, she saw him take a deep breath, his body tensing but his face calm. He was startled, yes, but not lost in the throes of a traumatic flashback.

Confusion swept over Aria. This was not the reaction she was used to. This was not the reaction she had braced herself for. She felt a knot of anxiety in her stomach, a familiar fear that had been triggered by the loud noise. Looking at Jace, seeing his steady gaze and calm demeanor, something inside her began to unwind.

She let out a breath she didn't know she'd been holding. She was still shaken, but she felt a glimmer of hope. Perhaps this time, things could be different. Perhaps this time, the past didn't have to repeat itself. And perhaps, just perhaps, she could learn to trust again.

His hand found hers across the table, a solid, reassuring presence that was like a balm to her frayed nerves. She knew her fears were rooted in the past, in experiences with someone who wasn't Jace. In this moment, she knew that her fears were her own demons that still had hold of her.

Aria would not remember the rest of the date. She was far too focused on saying the right thing, giving off the correct facial expressions, keeping her shoulders relaxed and not hunching from the tension.

But Jace knew. Of course, he knew. And he must be regretting his decision to ask her out.

She declined dessert or coffee. She made herself laugh when Jace made a joke about not trusting any caffeinated beverage not made by her hand. But her laugh was a feeble thing.

The cool night air slapped her in the face, making her realize they were walking to the car. The seat warmer in his car left her feeling cold. The silence that hung between the driver's and passenger seat told Aria that this thing between her and Jace was over before it had a true chance to start.

Aria didn't know what to say to him. She wasn't sure what to tell herself. She was still shaken by the whole incident. Not just the waiter's mishap with the tray. She was shaken by her instant attraction to Jace. By her attempt to open up to him. But mostly by the realization that she was still traumatized by her experiences with her first love.

Aria rubbed her hand over her brow. It came away damp. Was that sweat or tears?

Her gaze fixed outside the window as they drove by the beach she loved. She was lost in thought, her mind replaying the moments of the evening, the laughter they'd shared, the gentle touch of Jace's hand on hers, and the way his eyes seemed to light up when he looked at her.

She couldn't help but wonder what it would be like to kiss him, to feel his lips against hers. The thought made her heart race because she wanted those things. Wanted them with this man who she was surprised to realize she trusted to open herself to.

She'd been slashed open tonight with a clatter of silverware. She'd been shown that inside of herself, she wasn't ready to receive those things.

As Aria sat across from Jace, the realization hit her like a punch to the gut. It wasn't Jace who was dealing with PTSD; it was her. All this time, she had been so focused on her ex-husband's struggles, his triggers, his nightmares that she had ignored her own. She had borne the weight of his trauma, carrying it with her even after their relationship ended.

She looked into Jace's steady, patient eyes and felt a pang of regret. He was so different from her ex, so calm and collected. He had his demons, yes, but he was handling them with a grace and strength that she admired. As much as she wanted to explore the connection between them, she knew she had to deal with her own trauma first.

Aria looked up at him and felt a sense of loss. She was giving up on a chance at happiness, on a chance at love. But she knew it was the right thing to do. She needed to heal, to confront her own demons.

Jace turned to her, looking every bit the warrior, ready to vanquish any threat. What would he do when he realized that she was the enemy? The streetlights danced in his eyes, highlighting the concern etched in his features. The words she needed to say hung heavy in the air between them, a barrier she knew she had to breach.

"I'm sorry," she said when Jace pulled to a stop in front of her place.

"I'm not."

"I thought I was ready."

"I'll wait."

Aria didn't know what to say to this man. She had waited for her husband, and that waiting had been in vain. She couldn't ask Jace to wait for her to finish her healing.

"I can't ask that," she said, her words coming out in a rush. "I can't bear the thought of you waiting in vain... like I did with my ex."

Jace's expression softened, the furrows in his brow smoothing out. His silence was an invitation for her to continue, a quiet acceptance that he would listen to her, no matter what she had to say.

"I waited for him to get better," Aria confessed, her gaze dropping to her hands. "I waited, and I hoped, and I prayed. But it never happened. And it nearly broke me."

She looked up at Jace again, finding understanding in his gaze. But also in his gaze, she saw that he was still battle-ready. He wasn't getting the fact that she was trying to cut him loose.

"I can't do that to you, Jace. I can't ask you to wait for something that might never come. It's not fair to you."

"Aria..." Jace began, but she shook her head, cutting him off.

"No, Jace," she said firmly. "I care about you too much to put you through that. You deserve someone who can be fully present with you, who isn't haunted by the past."

The silence that followed was deafening. A dog walked its human down the street in a late-night stroll. It stopped at intervals, sniffing trees and bushes and poles and leaving messages for its friends. An owl hooted overhead, calling to its life-long mate. Insects scuttled about in the grasses, rubbing their legs together, signaling they were ready for a date. Aria felt her heart pounding in her chest, the echo of her words still ringing in her ears.

"Don't waste your time with me," she said as she opened the car door and raced inside her home.

CHAPTER TEN

Jace's hands were tightly clenched around the smooth rocks he had gathered from the shore. The rhythmic sound of the waves crashing against the shore provided a comforting white noise that helped to ground him. But it was sand beneath his feet, not solid earth.

His gaze fixed on the rolling waves, but his mind was in turmoil. The sand beneath him felt unstable, mirroring the uncertainty he felt in his heart. Aria's decision not to date him had shaken his sense of stability, leaving him restless and searching for a way to win her back.

He traced his fingers through the soft grains of sand, contemplating his next move. His mind raced with thoughts of how to prove himself worthy of Aria's love and trust. He knew he had to find a way to break down the walls she had built, to show her that he was different from her past experiences.

The sun continued its morning stretch over the horizon, casting a warm glow over the beach. The breeze rustled through his hair, stirring his thoughts. But he kept coming back to one singularity; he wanted Aria in his life.

She was the puzzle piece he hadn't known he was missing. She was the calm in his storm, even though the turmoil was brewing inside her. He wanted to help her. He just wasn't sure how.

He sipped at the bottled tea he'd purchased from the convenience store. It was only his good manners that had him not spitting it out. The tea tasted nothing like Aria's brew. It was filled with chemicals and too much sugar. It didn't have her personal touch that calmed the frayed edges of his nerves.

"Thought I'd find you here."

Jace looked over his shoulder to find Alex coming toward him. It took Jace a moment to recognize him. Alex was a serious man, always dressed impeccably. But he had his shoes off and was walking barefoot in the sand toward Jace.

"Figured I'd find you out here," Alex said. "Last few days of freedom before you're a clock puncher like the rest of us."

Jace would begin working at the base on Monday. His R&R would officially come to a close. But he felt like he'd barely gotten his feet under him.

"Why do I get the feeling you're not moping because you're headed back into the workforce?"

It was Mason who was the more perceptive one of their bunch. Even when his head was mostly in a book, Mason had a knack for reading between the lines. Alex was a numbers guy. He searched the data and often missed emotional cues. But Jace supposed he was very transparent in this moment, his feelings written all over his face.

"Did your date with the coffee maker not go as planned?"

"No," admitted Jace. "That was not how I planned last night to go."

"Buddy, if she's unwilling to be with you because of your past, then-"

"No, it's not my issues she's afraid of. It's her own," Jace confessed, his voice filled with disappointment. "Aria's been through a lot with her ex-husband's PTSD. Originally, I thought it would affect her ability to trust soldiers, including me. But she's still hurting from trying to support him."

Alex nodded, his expression sympathetic. "PTSD can have a profound impact on relationships. It's not easy for either party involved. Have you considered suggesting that Aria seek out a support group? They have some on the base. It could provide a safe space for her to share her experiences with other men and women who've been in her situation."

Jace leaned back on his arms, mulling over Alex's suggestion. It made sense. Aria needed to know that she wasn't alone in her struggles, and connecting with others who had gone through similar situations might offer her a fresh perspective. That was, if he could get her to talk to him again.

"Same goes for you, too," Alex continued. "You've been walking this beach for the past couple of weeks all by yourself. But you don't have to do it alone either."

Jace took a moment to process Alex's words. The idea of joining a support group had crossed his mind before, but he had been hesitant to take that step. He was already having trouble sitting still now that he was out of the service. Sitting still and talking about his feelings to strangers seemed a tall order.

"I joined a PTSD support group when I came to work on the base. At first, I did it to score points with command. But then, as I sat there listening to other men and women like me, it began to help. I saw that I wasn't alone. I saw that my experiences weren't unique. Others had gone through them and come out the other end better. Now I look at it as one of the best decisions I've ever made."

Once again, his friend surprised him. Alex was so analytical that Jace hadn't thought the man could hold a conversation with another person that wasn't tactical.

Alex took a deep breath, his gaze drifting toward the horizon. "Sharing my experiences with others who have gone through similar struggles has been incredibly healing. In that safe space, I've found understanding, empathy, and a sense of belonging that I didn't think was possible."

Jace leaned in, his interest growing. "What's it like? I mean, what do you talk about?"

"We talk about everything. Our experiences in the military, the challenges we face daily, and how our time in the service affects our lives today. But it's not just about sharing the difficult moments. We also celebrate victories, offer support, and provide guidance based on what has helped us individually."

Jace's gaze shifted to the waves crashing against the shore, contemplating Alex's words. "And you think it would help Aria?"

Alex's hand came down on Jace's shoulder. "I think it'll help both of you. It'll help you separately, and it could help you come together."

The fact that Jace put Aria's happiness before his own was just another clue to how deep his feelings for the woman were growing. If it weren't for her, he might spend the rest of his days walking this beach alone, searching for solace. But he'd found it in her smile, in her laugh, in the very air she breathed.

Last night when she'd looked so lost and a bit broken, Jace wanted to move heaven and earth to make her smile again. To see that twinkle in her eye. He would do anything to make that happen for her.

He knew how deeply rooted she was in their hometown community, relying on familiar faces and comfort. But he also recognized the limita-

tions of that community when it came to understanding the complexities of PTSD. Aria had been
the one to coax him out of his shell, encouraging
him to participate in the town events and connect
with others. She had shown him the power of
community, and now it was his turn to help her
see the potential benefits of joining a support
group.

CHAPTER ELEVEN

*A*ria sat behind the counter of her café, her gaze drifting toward the door with every jingle of the bell. Each time, her heart skipped a beat, hoping to see Jace stepping through the entrance, his lopsided, unpracticed grin lighting up the room. But time and time again, her anticipation turned into disappointment as familiar faces that she'd known all her life greeted her instead.

The realization that Jace might not be coming back sank in, weighing heavily on Aria's heart. Doubts gnawed at her, questioning whether she had made the right decision in letting him go. She missed his presence, the way he made her feel alive and understood. The café felt emptier without him, void of the energy and connection they had shared.

She found herself lost in memories, replaying their conversations, the tender moments they had shared. Aria remembered the vulnerability in Jace's eyes, the way he had opened up to her about his struggles and fears. She had seen the strength and determination within him, and she admired his courage in facing his demons head-on.

But the fear of being hurt resurfaced, whispering doubts into Aria's mind. The pain of her past experience with her ex-husband lingered, a reminder of the emotional turmoil that had left scars on her heart. She questioned whether she had the strength to go through it all again, the uncertainty of loving someone whose demons haunted them.

The soft chime of the doorbell pulled Aria out of her thoughts. Disappointment didn't weigh down her heart this time when she spotted the person who crossed the threshold into her establishment. It warmed her to see Sarah entering her café.

Sarah had called to check in on Aria after her date. When Aria was slow to spill the details, she had hung up and come over. Grace had let her in, and the two had surrounded Aria until she fessed up.

Both her friends had been there through the tumultuous years of Aria's marriage, witnessing firsthand the pain and struggles she had endured. Their bond ran deep, built on a foundation of trust and shared experiences.

"Hey, Sarah," Aria greeted, her voice tinged with a mix of gratitude and weariness. "You want your usual?"

Sarah walked up to the counter, her eyes filled with concern as she took in Aria's slightly downcast expression. "I want to know how you're holding up."

Aria sighed, her shoulders slumping as she leaned against the counter. "Honestly, it's been hard. I'm wavering, and it's only been a day."

Sarah reached out, gently placing her hand on top of Aria's. "I understand your fears, Aria. But I saw you with Jace. It looked different. He is different. He's shown you nothing but kindness and understanding. Even when he got bossy at the beach cleanup."

Aria's gaze dropped to the tabletop, her mind grappling with conflicting emotions. The memory of Jace's kindness, his protective nature during the beach cleanup, and the undeniable connection they had shared replayed in her thoughts. Sarah's words resonated, reminding her of the possibility of happiness that awaited if she dared to be vulnerable. She'd been taken aback by his initial stance of giving orders at the cleanup. Then his quick action when things took a turn for the worse. And there was that time in between when he faced down those messy college kids with just a glare and a few words.

Aria looked into Sarah's eyes, searching for reassurance. "But what if it's too soon? What if I'm not ready to take that leap of faith?"

Sarah squeezed Aria's hand, her voice filled with compassion. "Only you can decide when you're ready. I just want to make sure you're not letting fear hold you back from something that could be special."

"Says the woman who's sworn off men."

Sarah held up a finger. "I've sworn off cheating losers. If a real man who was responsible and loyal showed up, I'd consider changing my mind. But I don't see any of those around. Unless, that is, you wanna loan me Jace?"

Aria narrowed her gaze at her oldest friend.

Sarah let out a giggle. "That's what I thought."

A little jealousy was one thing. Committing to giving a relationship with Jace a try was another. "I don't want to let fear dictate my life. I want to give Jace a chance to explore what we could have together. But I'm scared, Sarah. Scared of getting hurt again."

"I understand your fear, but remember"—Sarah gave Aria's hand a comforting squeeze—"I also know that love has a way of healing wounds and filling the spaces that were once empty. Take it slow, communicate, and let yourself be vulnerable. You have the strength to navigate this, Aria. And I'll be here to support you every step of the way."

As she let her friend embrace her, Aria felt a renewed sense of hope, her heart whispering that perhaps it was time to let love back into her life. The day went by swiftly after that. Aria attended to her customers with a smile, her warmth masking the ache within. But deep down, she couldn't deny the void that had settled in her soul. She longed for Jace's presence, his understanding, and the way he made her feel seen.

"Excuse me, are you Aria?"

The person asking was an older woman Aria had never met. The town was big enough that not everyone knew everyone. The beach attracted tourists wanting some sandy fun where there was no access to oceans. And there was the base that had people coming and going.

"I am. Can I get you a warm beverage?"

"Actually, that would be nice, too. I'm here to reserve a pavilion on the beach. I'm told you're the person to speak to about that."

"I am. You'll just need to fill out a form. I can grab it for you. What's the event?"

"I run a support group for the loved ones of service members who suffered from PTSD."

Aria's fingers trembled as she handed over the clipboard with the necessary documents. Her gaze locked on the woman's. There was something in her pale eyes that told Aria she knew exactly what she'd gone through.

The urge to spill her guts was so powerful that Aria had to gulp down the words. She didn't know this woman. She was a stranger. But something inside Aria told her that wasn't true.

"My name is Faith. My husband lost his struggles battling PTSD. Since then, I've devoted my life to helping other men and women who loved someone with this disease."

Aria could only nod. Her throat was choked

with emotion and the need to shout and scream and cry all at the same time.

"We welcome new members, and if you know anyone who might need to talk to others who would understand what they're going through, we'd love to have them."

"You would?" Aria managed.

"Yes." Faith covered Aria's hand with her own. "Yes, we would. In fact, that's why we're holding the next meeting on the beach. We decided we need to publicize what we offer to let other people in the community know that we exist and we're here to listen."

"I think other people in the community would find what you do very helpful."

"I'm glad you think so. When Jace recommended a beach event, I was skeptical at first-"

"Jace?"

"Hmm. Jace Hunter. Do you know him?"

Did Aria know him? That man. Aria couldn't help the smile that started at the corner of her mouth. Yet again, he was trying to boss her around. On her own beach. This time, she just might let him take the lead.

CHAPTER TWELVE

J ace stood on the beach, a sense of nervous anticipation bubbling within him. Faith had given him the tasks of setting up chairs and arranging pamphlets for the support group event. He performed his orders, but his gaze wandered, searching for Aria among the gathering crowd.

A quarter of an hour before the event was set to start, she was nowhere to be seen. Doubts began to creep into his mind, and he couldn't help but worry that he had pushed too hard, too soon.

The truth was it was going to be hard for him to hold back. Even if she didn't come to this event, he had already determined that he wasn't giving up on her. He would make himself a regular at the coffee shop.

Just as soon as this event was over, he was going to go in and order a cup of the special tea she'd made for him. Then he'd return in the morning to order another before his first day of work. Sandy Perk would be where he'd spend his lunch break. And he'd be sure and stop by after work for a wind-down tea.

His mission was to win her over one cup at a time.

Jace's gaze swept across the beach again. This time, it landed on a familiar face. Michael, his partner from the beach cleanup, stood among the attendees of the support group. Their eyes met, a silent acknowledgement passing between them.

Making his way toward Michael, Jace offered a sympathetic smile. "Hey, man," he said softly, his voice filled with understanding. "I didn't expect to see you here."

Michael returned the smile, though a hint of weariness lingered in his eyes. "Yeah, my mom, she struggled with depression after her deployments. It had a negative impact on my dad, but I didn't realize it impacted me too."

"It's a heavy burden, loving someone who's

been through the challenges of service," said Jace. "But being here, supporting each other, is a step toward healing for all of you."

Michael's gaze shifted toward the group, where participants were engaged in heartfelt conversations. "I didn't know something like this existed until I saw it on the community billboard that Aria posted."

Just the mention of her name had Jace's heart skipping a beat.

"I used to feel so alone, like no one understood what it was like growing up in that environment," Michael confessed. "Being here, hearing others' stories, it gives me hope. And it makes me realize that I'm not alone on this journey."

A breeze lifted the tendrils of hair at the back of Jace's nape. The scent of lavender mixed with the salty sand. He knew she was here before he saw her. Then he turned, and all in the world felt right.

Aria strode toward him, a travel mug in each hand. When she reached him, she held out one to him.

"It's a peace offering," she said. "It's the peace tea I made for you the first time you came into my café."

Jace held the mug up to his nose. He inhaled the sweet scent, and it instantly settled any lingering tension in his body. That, and the sight of the woman standing before him.

"I was wrong to push you away the other night," she said.

"You were scared. I understand that."

"Oh? You're understanding enough that you organized a support group in my favorite place, hoping I'd show up?"

"Is that pushy?"

She smiled at him. That smile told him all he needed to know. She was going to try. She was going to give him a chance.

Jace reached out a hand to her. She took it with her free hand. But because he was a little pushy, he gave her a tug. She came to him, her chest coming flush with his. His heartbeat found hers and locked into step with its rhythm.

"I said I'd wait for you," said Jace. "I didn't say I'd be far away while I waited."

"I think I like you right where you are."

Their eyes locked, and in that instant, that magnetic surge of connection passed between them. Jace knew she felt it because he saw the vulnerability and love he felt reflected in Aria's gaze. It was an unspoken promise of support and understanding.

Jace dipped his head to Aria's and stole a kiss. Though stealing was the wrong word as she tilted her head back and offered him her lips. She tasted of honey and vanilla and peace and his. A warm breeze swept across the beach as Jace deepened the kiss.

Time seemed to stand still as they held each other, their embrace filled with a mixture of passion, hope, and the promise of a shared journey ahead. It was a kiss that carried the weight of their pasts, but also the optimism of a future built on trust and love.

As they pulled back, their eyes locked once more, their smiles radiant and their hearts alight with newfound joy. Jace knew that their path might not always be smooth, but he was ready to face the challenges together, supporting each other every step of the way.

And so, with the taste of chamomile tea and the sweetness of their kiss lingering in the air, Aria and Jace turned to take their seats in the support group. The community of new friends and old surrounded them, ready to support them as they embarked on their happily ever after.

. . .

Don't miss the next book in the Honor Valley Romances!

When a wounded warrior and a small-town woman agree to a fake relationship, will their pretend love turn into the real thing?

When Alex, a Wounded Warrior trying to get promoted in the workplace meets Sarah, who needs a fake boyfriend for an upcoming family event, they hatch a plan to help each other out. But what starts out as a pretend relationship quickly turns into something more as Sarah and Alex navigate their inner and outer conflicts only to misstep and begin to fall in love.

With a pushy boss and nosy coworkers on Alex's side and an overbearing family intent on getting a ring on Sarah's finger on the other side, these two don't stand a chance. Follow along as Sarah and Alex navigate the ups and downs of their fake relationship before realizing that their feelings for each other are all too real. Will they be able to overcome their fears and find true love, or will their pasts come back to haunt them?

Soldier's Promise is a heartwarming, small-town military romance that explores the power of love, growth, and healing. With the fake dating trope, wounded hero, and the love of family and community, this story will sweep you away and leave you rooting for Sarah and Alex's happily ever after.

ALSO BY SHANAE JOHNSON

Shanae Johnson was raised by Saturday Morning cartoons and After School Specials. She still doesn't understand why there isn't a life lesson that ties the issues of the day together just before bedtime. While she's still waiting for the meaning of it all, she writes stories to try and figure it all out. Her books are wholesome and sweet, but her are heroes are hot and heroines are full of sass!

And by the way, the E elongates the A. So it's pronounced Shan-aaaaaaaa. Perfect for a hero to call out across the moors, or up to a balcony, or to blare outside her window on a boombox. If you hear him calling her name, please send him her way!

You can sign up for Shanae's Reader Group and receive a FREE NOVELLA in this world at

https://shanaejohnson.com/ReaderGroup

ALSO BY SHANAE JOHNSON

Honor Valley Romances

Soldier's Surrender

Soldier's Promise

Soldier's Courage

Soldier's Embrace

Soldier's Protection

Soldier's Triumph

The Brides of Purple Heart

On His Bended Knee

Hand Over His Heart

Offering His Arm

His Permanent Scar

Having His Back

In Over His Head

Always On His Mind

Every Step He Takes

In His Good Hands

Light Up His Life

Strength to Stand

His Grace Under Pressure

The Rangers of Purple Heart

The Rancher takes his Convenient Bride

The Rancher takes his Best Friend's Sister

The Rancher takes his Runaway Bride

The Rancher takes his Star Crossed Love

The Rancher takes his Love at First Sight

The Rancher takes his Last Chance at Love

The Silver Star Ranch Romances

His Pledge to Honor

His Pledge to Cherish

His Pledge to Protect

His Pledge to Obey

His Pledge to Have

His Pledge to Hold

a Flying Cross Ranch Romance

His Vow to Love

His Vow to Treasure

His Vow to Adore

His Vow to Trust

His Vow to Respect

His Vow to Defend

Bronze Star Ranch Romance

His Duty to Serve

His Duty to Accept

His to Fulfill